Contents

Chapter One   7

Chapter Two   27

Chapter Three   37

Chapter Four   52

Chapter Five   73

Chapter Six   89

Chapter Seven   107

Chapter Eight   120

Chapter Nine   145

Chapter Ten   167

Chapter One

"Finished at last!" Sophie said, shutting her maths book in relief.

Her mum was standing at the sink, scrubbing potatoes for supper. "Homework done?"

Sophie nodded and pushed her blonde ponytail back over her shoulder. She

was in Year Six at Crosshills primary
school. It was great being at the top of
the school – she just didn't like all the
homework!

Max, her nine-year-old brother,
was colouring in a poster. "I've almost
finished my homework too," he said.

"Let's see." Sophie leaned over the
table. It was a poster advertising their
town. Max had drawn a picture of the
seafront and the little promenade with
the row of shops and restaurants that
looked out on to the beach. Under it
he'd written the words: Come to Easton-
on-Sea! It SHORE is the place to be!

"It's really good," said Sophie, admiring

the detail. "Is that Mr Franketelli sitting outside his restaurant?"

"Yep," said Max. Franketelli's was their family's favourite place to eat. It served the best pizzas ever! Mr Franketelli was old now and spent much of his time sitting under the green-and-white stripy awning outside the restaurant.

Sophie got up to help Mum with supper and spotted her baby sister, Lucie, pulling a sieve out of an open cupboard. Sophie hurried over. "No, that's not a toy, Lu-lu!" Lucie was just over a year old and super cute, with pale blonde hair and wide eyes, the same sky-blue as Sophie and Max's.

"Mine!" Lucie said firmly, her pudgy hand tightening on the handle. She put the sieve on her head and smiled. "Hat!"

Sophie giggled. "It's a very nice hat, Lucie. Now, why don't you come and sit in your high chair with your hat, and leave the cupboard alone?" She scooped her sister up off the floor.

"Thanks, Sophie," said her mum, throwing her a grateful look. "We really have to fix some child locks on the cupboards now that she's walking."

Sophie kissed her sister's soft hair. When Mum and Dad had first told her and Max they were going to have a baby sister, Sophie hadn't been too keen on

the idea. But now she couldn't imagine life without Lucie. "Shall I get her a rice cake?"

"Yes, please. That'll keep her quiet while I get these potatoes in the oven," said Mum.

"What time will Dad be home?" Sophie asked, as she fetched Lucie a rice cake. Dad managed The Wellington, a smart restaurant in town. He worked very long hours, but he usually tried to be home between shifts for an early dinner with the family. Her mum worked hard too – she was an accountant – but she was able to do quite a lot of her work from home.

"Soon," said Mum. "He's taking the night off."

"Why?" Sophie was surprised. Her dad almost never took a night off, apart from on Mondays when the restaurant was closed.

Mum tucked her blonde hair behind her ears. "It's our anniversary."

Sophie was confused. "But you're not married," she said. Her parents had never married, something she really didn't understand. *Who wouldn't want a wedding?* Sophie had been to one when she was six. She remembered the two bridesmaids wearing long pink dresses, lots of dancing and funny speeches. It had been

such a happy day. But her parents had
always said they didn't need a big day
to prove their love. "How can you have
an anniversary if you're not married?"
Sophie asked.

"It's the anniversary of when we first
met." Mum's eyes took on a far-away
look. "It was fifteen years ago today on
the beach." As she spoke, the back door
opened and Dad walked in – broad-
shouldered, dark-haired, blue eyes
twinkling.

"Fifteen years!" he declared. "And
I've loved every single one of them!" He
swept Mum up in a hug and kissed her.

"Ew! Gross!" Max pretended to be sick.

But Sophie grinned. She liked the fact that her parents were obviously still in love.

"Dada! Dada!" shouted Lucie, banging the sieve on her high chair table.

Dad walked over and scooped her out. "Fifteen years — so, tonight, my lovely family, we are going out to celebrate. I've booked us a table at Franketelli's."

Sophie squealed and Max whooped. "Pizza time!"

Mum looked anxious. "It's a nice idea, Tom, but I thought we agreed we wouldn't spend any extra money right now?" Sophie knew her parents were worried that The Wellington might close.

If that happened, her dad would lose his job.

"It's just one meal," Dad said. "Come on, Lizzie."

Mum frowned. "But—"

"Juicy tomatoes and creamy mozzarella," Dad interrupted. "Plump olives, crispy pizza bases, meatballs oozing with sauce . . ."

"Home-made ice cream!" Max added.

"Oh, please say we can go, Mum?"

"I-scream!" Lucie squealed.

Sophie put her hands together as if begging. "Please, Mum!"

Dad carried Lucie over and gave Mum a kiss on the cheek. "You have to say yes, Lizzie. How can you resist?"

The corners of Mum's mouth lifted into a smile as she gave in. "All right then. Yes!"

Half an hour later, the family parked their old blue people carrier and piled out in front of the restaurant. Mr Franketelli was sitting outside as usual,

enjoying the last few rays of the summer
sun. His face was deeply wrinkled, his
hair grey, but his eyes lit up when he saw
the Jenkins family.

"*Buono sera,* my friends!" he said,
getting up from his chair and opening
his arms wide. "Welcome! Welcome! It
is so lovely to see you again!" He spoke
with a strong Italian accent.

Mr Franketelli kissed Mum on both
cheeks, asked Dad about his work and
then showed them to their table. The
restaurant had been open for many
years and was always busy. The walls
were covered with photographs of
southern Italy, where Mr Franketelli had

been born. The red carpet was old and faded, and the green paint on the walls scuffed. But it didn't matter, because the restaurant smelt delicious and the chequered tablecloths were cheery. As usual, there was a pot of breadsticks in the centre of their table.

Max took one and wielded it like a weapon. "Gimme some dough!" he said to Dad.

"Or what? You wanna *pizza* this?" Dad grabbed another breadstick for a sword-fight.

"Remind me how many children I have?" Mum said to Sophie, shaking her head.

The family sat down and ordered. Soon they were tucking into bowls of meatballs and homemade pasta for Mum and Dad, margarita pizza for Max and Sophie, and breadsticks and vegetables for Lucie.

After ten minutes, Lucie got bored and began to throw the breadsticks on the floor. Franketelli's was so relaxed that no one minded. Mr Franketelli's cheerful wife, Gina, came and took Lucie over to the window to look at the seagulls.

Mum sighed happily. "I do love it here."

Dad squeezed her hand. "Happy anniversary."

"No more soppiness!" begged Max, as Mum leaned over to kiss Dad. "Look! I've got a new magic trick," he added hastily. Max loved doing magic and spent as much time as he was allowed watching videos of tricks. He pulled a ten pence coin out of his pocket and held it out on his palm. "Now you see it." He held out his other hand which was empty. "And now you don't." He closed his fists, then tapped them together twice. "Abracadabra!" He opened his hands again and revealed a ten pence coin in both hands. "I've doubled my money!"

"Now, *that* is a good trick!" said Mum.

Dad grinned. "Yes, definitely not a

trick to . . ." he paused, "CHANGE!"

Dad and Max fist-bumped while Sophie and Mum groaned.

"So, what have you been up to today, Soph?" Dad said.

"Just lessons, really. And swimming this morning." Sophie was on the swim team at the local pool and got up early before school two days a week to train.

"When's your next gala?" Dad asked.

"Next month," Sophie said. "Oh, and I joined a new club at school today ," she remembered. "Drama."

"Another club?" Mum said. "You must have one every day of the week now."

"Yep!" said Sophie happily.

"Can we have ice cream for pudding?" Max begged.

"We can indeed," said Dad.

Max and Sophie high-fived, knocking the salt cellar off the table. "Whoops!" said Max.

"Don't worry, I'll get it." Dad got off his chair and fumbled around under the tablecloth. "But before we order the ice cream," he said, his voice slightly muffled, "I have something to ask Mum." He emerged from under the table holding a breadstick high in the air. There was a diamond ring on the end of it, sparkling in the light. Sophie gasped. What did this mean? Was Dad about to . . . *propose?*

"Lizzie, you've put up with me for fifteen years," Dad said, gazing at Mum. "Will you marry me and stay with me forever?"

Mum's eyes grew wider and wider as she stared at the ring. The diners around them noticed what was going on and the clatter of cutlery and buzz of chatter stopped.

"Mum?" Sophie's voice came out in a squeak as her eyes flicked from her mum's face to her dad's. What was Mum going to say? For a moment, the world seemed to hold its breath.

An enormous smile spread across Mum's face. "Of course, I will!" she exclaimed.

Happiness exploded through Sophie. The watching diners cheered and Dad jumped to his feet. Sophie and Max were

instantly on their feet too, hugging their parents.

"Oh, wow! Wow! Wow!" Sophie cried.

Gina hurried over with Lucie to join in the family celebration. There was a loud pop and Mr Franketelli appeared with a bottle of champagne and glasses.

"*Splendido!*" he cried, as Dad slipped the engagement ring on Mum's finger. "*Magnifico!*" he poured the champagne with a flourish. "Dessert is on the house!"

Sophie's head spun. "Mum! You're going to get married!" she gasped, as Dad took Lucie from Gina and hugged Max.

"I can hardly believe it, but I am! I

really am!" Sophie didn't think it was possible to feel any happier. But then Mum took her hands, eyes shining with excitement. "Will you be my bridesmaid, Sophie?" she asked.

Sophie thought she would burst with joy. "Oh yes!" she squealed.

Chapter Two

"Guess what!" Sophie announced, as she arrived in her classroom the next morning. "My mum and dad are getting married and I'm going to be a bridesmaid!"

Her friends all hugged her, but after a brief flurry of questions the

conversation quickly moved on to the netball tournament next weekend.

Sophie dumped her bag on the floor and perched on her desk, feeling slightly deflated. She thought being a bridesmaid was amazing, but her friends didn't seem to share her excitement.

Shanti, one of the quieter girls in her class, came over. She had long dark hair and brown eyes framed by curling eyelashes.

"Hi," Sophie said.

Shanti looked at her shyly. "I heard what you just said . . . about being a bridesmaid. And . . . well . . . I'm going to be one, too!"

Sophie's eyes lit up. "Really? When? Who for?"

"For my big sister. She's getting married in a few months." Shanti's smile widened. "I'm so excited! I've never been a bridesmaid before."

"Me too!" said Sophie, glad to have found someone who shared her excitement.

"Cora and Emily are both going to be bridesmaids, too," said Shanti.

"Cora and Emily in Miss Dixon's class?"

Shanti nodded.

Sophie knew Emily from her after-school street dance class, and she and

Cora had been in the same gymnastics club when they were younger.

"Let's find them at breaktime. We can talk about weddings," Shanti suggested.

Sophie nodded eagerly.

Just then the bell rang.

"Meet me by the lockers," said Shanti. And with a final smile she returned to her desk on the far side of the class.

At breaktime, Sophie and Shanti hurried outside. Cora and Emily were already in the playground, sitting on a low wall. Cora had strawberry-blonde hair that curled under her chin and a

smattering of freckles across her nose
and cheekbones. Emily had dark curly
hair, pulled back into a ponytail, and big
brown eyes. Both girls looked surprised,
but Shanti quickly explained. "You'll
never guess what – Sophie's going to be
a bridesmaid, just like us. Her mum and
dad are getting married!"

"Oh, wow!" said Emily, staring at
Sophie. "Your actual mum and dad!"

"Yes, they never got round to getting married but my dad proposed last night," said Sophie. "At Franketelli's."

"I love that place!" said Cora.

"Their pizza's the best," said Shanti, nodding.

"How about you two? Who are you being bridesmaids for?" Sophie asked curiously.

Cora rolled her eyes. "My dad and Helena, his girlfriend." She didn't sound too impressed. "I want to be a bridesmaid and the wedding's going to be in this super-posh castle, but I don't want my dad to marry Horrible Helena."

"That's tough," said Sophie. It would be weird being a bridesmaid if you didn't like the bride.

"I'm going to be bridesmaid for my Uncle Josh," Emily said. She dropped her voice to a whisper. "No one at school knows this yet, but he's getting married to his boyfriend, Zack – Mr Taylor, Class 3T's teacher."

"I'll keep it secret," Sophie promised. She hadn't been taught by Mr Taylor, but he was running the drama club and seemed really nice. "How long have they been going out?"

"Three years," said Emily. "They're getting married in a smart hotel."

"Where are your parents getting married?" Cora asked Sophie.

"They haven't decided yet," said Sophie.

"Maybe it'll be at a hotel too," said Shanti.

"Or in a castle like my dad," said Cora.

Sophie grinned. "I don't mind so long as it's not in a football stadium! My dad loves football."

"A football wedding would be cool," said Cora. "Or a wedding at a stables – I love ponies."

"We could help you make a list of possible wedding places and you could show it to your parents," said Shanti,

pulling out a notebook. "After all, being a bridesmaid's not just about wearing a pretty dress. It's about helping organise the wedding and sorting out problems."

Emily gave a squeal. "That's just given me the best idea! We should form a club – a Bridesmaids Club. We could come up with ideas to help your parents decide on themes . . ."

"Oh, yes!" said Shanti. "We could help with things like flowers and decorations, too."

"Let's do it!" said Sophie.

Cora grinned. "Maybe you can all help me persuade my dad to marry someone else!"

The bell rang and they groaned.

"It can't be the end of break already," said Sophie. "There's so much more to talk about. When shall we meet next? I can't meet at lunchtime. I've got road safety club today. And I'm swimming after school."

"How about tomorrow breaktime," suggested Shanti.

They all nodded.

This is going to be so much fun, thought Sophie. "To Bridesmaids Club!" she said, holding her hand up.

They all met her hand in a high-five. "The Bridesmaids Club!" they echoed.

Chapter Three

As Sophie cycled into Tennison Road, she spotted a smart silver sports car parked on the driveway next to her mum and dad's old blue people carrier. Aunty Allie was visiting! Aunty Allie was her mum's younger sister. She was twenty-six and Sophie really liked her. *I bet she's here*

to talk about the wedding, Sophie thought excitedly. Last night, Mum had said that Aunty Allie was going to be her maid of honour, a kind of grown-up bridesmaid.

Wheeling her bike through the gate, Sophie left it in the shed and went in through the back door. Her mum and Aunty Allie were at the kitchen table, and Lucie was pushing some trains around the floor.

"Choo-choo!" Lucie was chuntering to herself. "Choo-choo . . ." She banged two trains together. "CRASH!" Lucie looked sadly at the jumble of carriages on the floor. "Uh oh!" Then she saw Sophie and her little face broke into a big smile.

"Soapy! Soapy's back!"

Sophie gave her sister a quick kiss. "Yes, Soapy's back."

"Hi, Soph," Aunty Allie said. Her shoulder-length blonde hair was swept up in a low bun and she was wearing smart trousers and a green shirt. She worked in an advertising agency. "Your mum told me the news about the wedding. Isn't it brilliant?"

Sophie beamed. "It really is!"

"How was school?" Mum asked.

"Just normal," said Sophie, sitting down beside her. She liked chatting with her mum about school when she got in, but today there were much more important

things to discuss! The table was covered with wedding magazines. "Have you decided where you want to get married yet?" she asked eagerly.

"Not yet," Mum admitted. "But we have applied for a marriage license."

Sophie picked up one of the magazines and flicked through the pages. "How about a hippy wedding? It could be like when you were young."

Her mum swatted her lightly. "I wasn't even born in the 1960s when there were hippies, thank you very much!"

Sophie turned the page and saw a bride in a woodland glade with the bridesmaids dressed as fairies. "OK, so

how about a fairy wedding in a wood?
Or a farm wedding in a barn? Or . . ."
she turned the page and grinned. "Hey,
Aunty Allie, if you were getting married,
this would be a wedding for you!" The
bride in the picture was wearing a black
and silver dress, a leather jacket and
ripped tights. The guests all had spiky
hair and were holding guitars up for the
bride and groom to walk through. "A
rock wedding!" said Sophie.

"I think not!" said Aunty Allie
grinning back at Sophie. "Though
Zayne might like the idea!" Aunty Allie's
boyfriend, Zayne, was in band and
always wore a leather jacket.

They leafed through the magazines together. There were so many different wedding themes – 1950s, disco, vintage, fairy-tale, gothic, garden party . . .

"Oh, I just don't know!" exclaimed Mum, as the back door opened and Dad came in with Max.

"What don't you know, my beautiful

bride-to-be?" he said.

"What type of wedding we should have," said Mum.

"Type of wedding?" Dad looked puzzled. "A wedding's just a wedding, isn't it?"

Sophie and her aunt swapped looks. "Did he seriously just say that?" said Aunty Allie, shaking her head.

"Wedding's usually have a theme, Dad," Sophie explained.

Dad raised his eyebrows at Max. "Do you understand this? It's all Greek to me."

"Ooh!" Sophie's eyes lit up. "Mum, maybe you could have an Ancient Greek

theme. Everyone could have ivy in their hair and wear goddess-style dresses . . ."

"Oh, yes! I'd look great in a goddess dress!" said Dad, posing with his hands on his hips and winking at Max.

"Dad!" Sophie complained, as Max chuckled. "You're not taking this seriously."

"I don't know what you're talking about." Dad nudged Max. "Hey, Max, did you hear about the notebook that married a pencil? She finally found her Mr Write!"

Max laughed while the rest of them groaned.

"Cup of tea everyone?" Dad asked,

putting the kettle on.

As he made the tea and got Lucie a biscuit, Mum, Sophie and Aunty Allie continued looking through the wedding magazines. Max joined them. "You could have a magic theme for your wedding," he suggested, wrapping his arms around Mum's neck.

"Maybe not magic," said Mum. "But it should be something special to me and your dad."

"What do both of you like?" asked Sophie.

"Each other!" called Dad.

"Not helpful, Dad," said Sophie. "Mum likes swimming and—"

"I know! We could re-enact the time we first met," said Dad. "Your mum could be on the beach in her wedding dress and I could stride out of the sea like James Bond."

Mum raised her eyebrows. "Except that's not really what happened, is it?"

"You were so bad at swimming, Dad, you almost drowned!" giggled Sophie. She loved hearing the story of how her mum and dad had first met, when her mum was a lifeguard on the beach. "You were trying to impress Mum so you jumped in from the rocks . . ."

"Yes, OK." Dad sighed. "I got cramp and she had to rescue me. More Mr

Bump than Mr Bond!" He brought the cups of tea over and kissed the top of Mum's head. "Your mum appeared like a mermaid and towed me back to the shore. Once we were on the beach I asked her to give me the kiss of life and—"

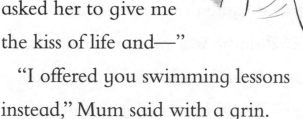

"I offered you swimming lessons instead," Mum said with a grin.

Luckily Dad had accepted the lessons, and they had fallen in love! There was a photo of them on the mantlepiece in

the lounge, taken soon after they had met – her mum with long, tousled hair, looking gorgeous in a red swimsuit and her dad in faded trunks that came down to his knees, skinnier than he was now but still broad-shouldered and handsome. They looked utterly in love with each other, the sun shining down and the waves behind them . . . Sophie gasped.

"I've got it! I know what type of

wedding you should have!"

"Yes?" said Aunty Allie eagerly.

"A beach wedding!" exclaimed Sophie.

"Oh, yes!" Mum clasped her hands together.

"I actually like that idea. Good one, Soph!" said Dad. "We could go abroad, maybe to the Caribbean – I've always wanted to go there."

"Zayne and I will come with you!" Allie said quickly.

Mum laughed. "We can't get married in the Caribbean, Tom. It would be much too expensive!"

"We could make it our honeymoon as well," said Dad.

"Please say yes, Mum!" begged Sophie.

"Yes, please, Mum!" added Max. "We could go swimming and snorkelling."

"It would be amazing!" said Sophie, picturing white sand and perfect turquoise water, and her parents barefoot, both in white, under an arch of bright tropical flowers.

"It's not a completely stupid idea, Lizzie," said Dad. "We could use the money we've been saving for a new car and what we would have spent on a holiday."

Mum looked tempted. "I suppose it would be wonderful." She looked at Allie. "You would definitely come too?"

"Of course!" Aunty Allie said. "And you know mum and dad love any excuse for a holiday."

"I'm sure my mum would come too," said Dad. "So, all the important people would be there."

Mum's face broke into a smile. "OK then," she said. Her words were drowned out by squeals and cheers. "Let's do it! Let's have a tropical wedding in the Caribbean!"

Chapter Four

"A tropical wedding! Oh, wow!"
breathed Shanti when Sophie told her
friends in the Bridesmaids Club the next
day. "Sun, sea, sand."

"You're so lucky!" said Emily.

Cora nodded. "You get to be
bridesmaid and have an amazing

holiday! How awesome is that?"

Sophie grinned. "I know!"

The four of them were sitting outside in the playground eating their breaktime snacks. "So, we don't need to help your parents decide where to have their wedding after all," said Emily. "But we could still make lists of all the things that need to be sorted out. Do you all want to come round to my house after school? We could watch some old episodes of *Here Comes The Bride.*"

Shanti and Cora nodded eagerly, but Sophie shook her head. "I can't tonight."

"Have you got swim practice?" Shanti asked her.

"No. I'm going wedding dress shopping with my mum and my aunt!"

The other three squealed in excitement.

"Oooh, take lots of photos," urged Shanti.

"Oh, I will," promised Sophie. Wedding dress shopping! She couldn't wait!

Aunty Allie was waiting in her car for Sophie after school. "Ready to shop till you drop?" she said, as Sophie pulled open the passenger door.

"It's all I've been thinking about!" Sophie said, throwing her bag inside. To her surprise, Max was there, sitting in

one of the small back seats, and Lucie too, fast asleep in her baby seat next to him.

"Dress shopping – yay!" said Max not sounding too keen.

Sophie frowned. "What's going on? I thought Dad was looking after you two."

"Your dad was called in for a meeting at work," said Aunty Allie, "so, I said I'd bring you all along to the fitting."

Max groaned. "It's going to be really girly, isn't it?"

"Don't worry. You can just sit on one of the sofas in the shop and play on my phone," Aunty Allie told him.

"Sofas? Is it a really posh shop?" said

Sophie, getting even more excited.

"Oh, yes!" said her aunt with a smile.

Sophie had never been in such a smart shop. It was called Wedding Belles and had a soft, duck-egg blue carpet and a glittering chandelier. Downstairs there were shelves of white bridal shoes, sparkling diamond headdresses and hats in all shapes and colours. An elegant sales assistant, called Valerie, checked them in using a big leather-bound diary and took them up a curving staircase.

"Elizabeth is here already," Valerie told them. "She's started to pick out a few dresses." Sophie grinned at her aunt. It was weird hearing her mum being called

by her full name. Everyone usually called her Lizzie.

"Look at all the dresses," Sophie said, as they reached the top of the stairs and found themselves in front of rails of beautiful white, ivory and cream wedding dresses. There were three velvet sofas, long mirrors and four changing rooms with dark blue curtains. Her mum was browsing through the rails. Hearing their footsteps, she turned. "Isn't this great?" she said, her eyes shining. "I've chosen two dresses to try on already!"

Aunty Allie put Lucie's car seat down on the floor and gave Max her phone to play with while Valerie got drinks for

everyone – juice for Max and Sophie, and glasses of sparkling wine for Mum and Aunty Allie.

"Feel free to start trying them on," Valerie said to Mum. "Don't be surprised if the first few aren't quite right. Wedding dresses often look very different on the hanger to how they look on. Once you've tried a few and I've got an idea of what might suit you, I'll make some suggestions. You were saying that it's going to be a beach wedding?"

Mum nodded. "We haven't quite decided exactly where."

"But somewhere hot," said Aunty Allie.

"So, you need a dress that can be

transported easily." Valerie ushered
Mum into one of the changing rooms.
As they waited for Mum to reappear,
Sophie went over to the rails and looked
through the dresses herself. There were
long ones and short ones, some made of
lace, others of delicate silk, shiny satin
and soft velvet. Some had big puffy skirts
and others were completely straight.
Which style would suit her mum? She
paused when she saw a long ivory dress
made from chiffon fabric and with a
halter neck. It was hard to imagine
exactly what it would look like on, but
she thought the skirt would be straight
and slightly floaty. Sophie had a feeling

the dress would really suit her mum.

Hearing muffled laughter coming from the changing room, Sophie turned as her mum came out in a cream lace dress. It was very long – the hem pooled around her feet – and it was so tight she could only walk with tiny steps.

"Well, what do you think?" Mum said, striking a pose. Lace clung to every inch of her body.

Sophie didn't know what to say. Her mum looked like a sausage! She

60

glanced at Aunty Allie and saw she was
also staring at Mum with a look of
barely-disguised horror.

Her mum burst out laughing. "It's OK.
I know it looks awful! I'll try another
one."

Sophie let out a sigh of relief as her
mum went back into the changing room.
"What do you think of this dress?" she
called to Aunty Allie who was getting
a rice cake out of the changing bag for
Lucie who had just woken up. Sophie
pushed the other dresses on the rail back
so her aunt could see the one with the
halter neck.

"It looks a bit shapeless," her aunt said,

glancing over. "But it might look nice on."

There was the sound of laughing from behind the curtain again. "Oh, my gosh, that's the *front?*" Sophie heard her mum saying. "No, no. It's OK. I'll keep it on and show it to them."

Mum came out, her eyes twinkling. "Well?"

Sophie, Aunty Allie and Max all burst out laughing. The dress had a puffy skirt and an extremely deep V at the front slashed all the way to Mum's tummy button. "I thought this was the back of the dress," said Mum, holding the front so it didn't gape open across her chest.

"So, what do you think?"

Lucie spat out her rice cake.

"I think that's definitely a no from Lucie!" said Sophie with a grin, as Aunty Allie grabbed a muslin cloth.

"How about this one?" Sophie showed her mum the dress she liked.

"It's a bit plain," her mum said doubtfully. "But I might as well try it." She took the dress off the rail and went back into the changing room.

She was in there for longer this time. Sophie waited for the sound of laughter, but there wasn't any.

"What's it like, Mum?" she called.

The curtain pulled back and her mum

stepped out. "Well? What do you think?" she said almost shyly.

"Oh!" Sophie gasped. The dress was absolutely perfect. The bodice fitted her mum like a glove and the floaty chiffon skirt fell to the floor in soft folds.

"You look like a princess, Mum!" said Max.

Valerie came out of the changing room. "It's a perfect dress for a beach wedding. It has a detachable train. Let's see how it looks on."

"And a veil and shoes too?" asked Sophie eagerly.

"Oh, I don't need to bother about those things yet," Mum said.

"No, your daughter is right," said Valerie firmly. "She's clearly a natural at this. You need to see the full effect."

Ten minutes later, Mum's wedding outfit was complete.

"I can't wear a tiara," she protested, as Valerie fixed a jewelled headband on her hair. "I'm not a princess."

"You will be on your wedding day," said Valerie, attaching a veil to the tiara. Then she hooked the train on to the back of the dress. "Now, Sophie, I assume you are the bridesmaid. It'll be your job to carry your mum's train and make sure it's spread out perfectly behind her when the ceremony takes place."

Sophie hurried round behind Mum and picked up the edges of the train. As Mum walked forward slowly, Sophie followed behind her holding up the train. In her imagination, they weren't in the shop, but on a beach with a bright blue sky and palm trees.

"You look incredible," said Aunty Allie, tears in her eyes.

"Mama, mama, mama," chanted Lucie.

Even Max was beaming. "You can wear *that* dress, Mum," he said. "I like it."

Mum stopped walking and looked at herself in the mirror. Her smile broadened. "I really like it too,' she said. "In fact, I love it!" She checked the price

tag that was attached to the skirt and frowned. "But it is a lot of money."

"Treat yourself, Lizzie" said Aunty Allie. "You should have the dress of your dreams on your wedding day."

Mum hesitated and then nodded. "I'll take it!" she told Valerie.

They were all smiling as they left the shop. "Thank you for making me buy it," Mum said, hugging Aunty Allie as they said goodbye to her. "You're right. It's perfect!"

"That was so much fun," said Sophie.

"Next, we'll have to find you a

bridesmaid dress!" said Mum.

They talked about dresses all the way home. Sophie was brimming with happiness as they let themselves into the house. "Dad's home," she said, noticing his coat and bag in the hall.

"That's strange," said Mum. "I thought he'd be at work." She carried Lucie through to the kitchen. Sophie followed her while Max went to put the TV on.

Dad was sitting at the kitchen table. Sophie immediately knew something was wrong. He didn't jump up to greet them or give them a hug like he usually did. He just turned to look at them and his face was full of worry, the twinkle

missing from his eyes.

"Tom?" Mum said, frowning. "Is everything OK?"

Dad let out a long, shaky breath. "Things have definitely been better."

"Why? What's happened?" asked Mum.

"Dad?" said Sophie.

"The meeting I went to this afternoon . . . Well, it was about the restaurant," Dad said, looking at Mum. "It's closing down, Lizzie. I've lost my job."

"Oh no," breathed Mum.

"Oh, Dad!" Sophie gave him a hug. "You'll find another job," she told him.

"Sophie's right," said Mum, sitting down beside him and taking his hand.

"Something else will come along. We'll just have to tighten our belts for a while and not spend any money until you've found another job."

Sophie saw her parents exchange a look. A horrible thought crossed her mind. "You will still get married though, won't you?" she asked them.

"I think we'd better put the wedding plans on hold," said Mum. "Not forever," she added quickly. "Just until Dad finds a new job and things have settled down."

Dad nodded. "There's not going to be enough money for a trip abroad right now. Maybe next year."

Disappointment flooded through Sophie. Next year! But her friends in Bridesmaids Club were all going to be bridesmaids soon. Now, she was going to be the odd one out, the only one who had to wait. Her heart sank into her toes.

Next year was ages away!

Chapter Five

"Oh, Sophie! That's awful!" Shanti exclaimed when Sophie told her the news at school the next day. "I'm so sorry!"

"I can't believe I'm not going to be a bridesmaid this year," Sophie said, swallowing.

"You're still going to be one though, and that's the main thing," Shanti comforted her. "Look, I think we need a meeting of the club to cheer you up. I'll check with my mum when I get home from school and see if the others can come over too."

That day, time seemed to drag. Sophie couldn't concentrate on anything her teacher was saying. Even during PE, normally her favourite lesson, she couldn't stop worrying about Dad, and the wedding.

But when she got home from school, there was a message on her phone from Shanti.

C and E can come round too. C U at mine! My mum's baked biscuits! xox

Sophie's tummy rumbled. She wasn't sure her Bridesmaids Club friends would be able to cheer her up, but she liked the sound of home-made biscuits!

Shanti's house was just a short bike ride from Sophie's. She lived on a modern housing estate and Sophie found her house easily. It had a large double garage and a wide, paved driveway at the front of the house with a neat patch of lawn edged by a low hedge. Sophie left her bike at the side of the garage

and knocked on the door. Shanti pulled it open. Cora and Emily were already there. They surrounded Sophie and hugged her.

"It's horrible about your dad's job," said Emily.

"And having to put the wedding off," said Cora.

"But even if your mum and dad don't get married for a while, you're definitely still part of the Bridesmaids Club," said Shanti.

Sophie hardly ever cried but her friends were being so nice, she could feel her eyes prickle with tears. She blinked them back. "Thanks. I guess I'll just have

to concentrate on all your weddings for now."

"Or . . ." Cora's eyes widened. "Maybe we can do something to make your mum and dad's wedding go ahead anyway!"

Sophie sighed. "I don't think there's anything we can do."

"There might be," said Shanti. "Let's go to my room and see if we can think of something."

Just then, Shanti's mum came out of the kitchen. Sophie recognised her from the playground at home time. She had shiny black hair that curled under at her shoulders and a wide smile just like Shanti's. She was wearing jeans and a

bright-turquoise blouse, and was holding a plate of chocolate chip cookies. "Here you go girls. These should keep you going until supper."

"Thanks, Mum!" said Shanti.

Sophie followed Shanti and the others upstairs. Shanti's room was the first door off the landing. It was small, but very tidy. The walls were painted white and the window had purple curtains with large pink flowers that matched the cushions on the bed. Under the window was a little white desk with a neat stack of books, pencils and pens carefully arranged in a pot, and flavoured lip glosses lined up in a row. On the outside

of the wardrobe hung a dark pink silk skirt with a gold hem and gold embroidery over it.

"Oh, wow, is that yours?" said Sophie, distracted from her unhappiness. She went closer and carefully touched the soft silk fabric.

"Yes, it's the *lehenga* I'm wearing when I'm a bridesmaid," said Shanti.

"It's gorgeous," said Sophie.

"My gran in India just sent it over for my sister's wedding." Shanti smiled. "The wedding's not for weeks, but she likes to be prepared!"

Emily grinned and took a cookie. "Just like you!"

"My mum found a wedding dress yesterday. She bought it, but maybe she'll return it now the wedding's been put off," Sophie said sadly.

"There's got to be something we can do to help," said Cora.

"I don't think there is," sighed Sophie, munching on a biscuit. "There's no way Mum and Dad will be able to pay for an

expensive beach wedding abroad while he doesn't have a job."

Cora frowned. "But they don't need to go abroad to have a beach wedding, do they? Couldn't they just have one on the beach here in Easton? It would be much cheaper."

"Yes," said Emily. "They wouldn't have to pay for a hotel or anything. And the cake and decorations could be home-made."

A flicker of excitement grew inside Sophie. Her friends were right. You didn't have to go abroad to have a beach wedding, did you? "If they got married on the beach here, they'd be getting

married where they met."

"That would be so romantic!" exclaimed Shanti.

"We could make the decorations for them," said Emily. "I love making things and my dad can get loads of supplies from the craft shop he works at."

"We could organise it all between us so your parents wouldn't have to worry," said Shanti.

"It could be a surprise!" said Sophie.

"We could do the flowers," said Emily, "and bake a wedding cake ..."

"Actually, I bet my gran would do that," said Sophie. "She loves baking."

"And your mum's already got a dress,"

said Cora. "This could work, Sophie!"

Sophie felt her excitement growing. "Why don't I phone my aunt and see what she thinks?"

Sophie video-called her Aunty Allie. To her delight, she seemed to love the idea of a surprise wedding! "Your mum had a surprise party for her sixteenth birthday and she always said it was the best party ever," said Aunty Allie.

"It could be outside on the beach!" said Sophie.

"Or what about the bandstand?" suggested Aunty Allie.

"Opposite Franketelli's?" said Sophie in excitement, thinking of the pretty

Victorian bandstand that stood at the end of a short pier that jutted off the promenade. "Yes, that would be perfect." She imagined the ornate metal pillars and canopy decorated with flowers and fairy lights. "We could have the wedding there at sunset, and go for pizza and ice cream at Franketelli's afterwards!"

"Brilliant idea!" said Aunty Allie. "In fact, we could tell your parents I'm having my birthday party at Franketelli's. They'll turn up and find they're at their own wedding! Oh, Sophie. This is genius!"

Sophie turned the phone towards

Shanti, Cora and Emily. "Aunty Allie, these are my friends. They want to help me organise it. We're the Bridesmaids Club."

"Hi!" They all waved into the camera.

"Hi, girls," said Aunty Allie. "Now, are you all quite sure about organising this? I can do the stuff you need a grown up for, but I'm really busy with work right now, so there's no way I can organise the whole thing. And Sophie can't do it on her own."

"We'd love to do it!" said Emily.

"We can make lists!" said Shanti waving a notebook. "We can sort everything out. The invitations, the flowers, the cake, the decorations, the bridesmaid dress . . ."

"The entertainment!" said Cora.

"No need to worry about that," said Aunty Allie. "I can get my boyfriend's band to play. And I bet Max would like to do some magic tricks, Sophie."

She nodded. "Oh yes!" She could imagine how delighted Max would be to perform.

"OK, tell you what, let's have it on my birthday – which is in just two and a half weeks. The weather should still be warm enough. I'll pay for the food as my wedding gift to your mum and dad. I'll have a word with Mr Franketelli and

see what deal he'll do us," said Aunty Allie. "Franketelli's is usually closed on Mondays so he won't be losing any regular business. I'll make sure he knows it's a surprise. I can print out some invitations at work and book someone to conduct the marriage ceremony. But I'll leave everything else up to you lot for now."

Sophie grinned. "This is going to be so much fun!"

"We'd better get on with organising things," said Shanti.

Aunty Allie nodded. "There's not a moment to waste!"

As soon as Sophie ended the call,

everyone started to talk at once.

"The Bridesmaids Club's very own secret wedding!" whooped Cora. "Bring it on!"

Chapter Six

"Mum, the post's here," said Sophie, picking the mail up from the doormat a few days later. She saw a thick cream envelope among the pile of brown boring ones and smiled to herself before carrying it all through to the kitchen. Her dad was on his laptop searching for

jobs while Max and Mum were tidying up after a Saturday morning brunch of bacon, sausages and egg. Lucie was having a nap in her cot upstairs.

"Thanks, sweetie. Just bills and more bills," her mum sighed, leafing through the envelopes that Sophie had handed her. "Wait, what's this?" She held up the cream envelope. "It looks like Allie's writing." She ripped the top of the envelope open and pulled out a cream card. "Gosh. Allie's having a

birthday party at Franketelli's."

"Really?" said Sophie, acting surprised although she had helped Aunty Allie send the invitations out!

"Yes, two weeks on Monday. We're all invited. I wonder why she didn't say anything when we saw her at the wedding dress shop . . ."

"Who knows, but it sounds fun and we could definitely use something to look forward to," said Dad.

Sophie saw Max grinning. She'd told him about the surprise wedding and he was already busy practising some magic tricks. She frowned and gave him a warning shake of her head as

she realised he was about to laugh. He clapped a hand over his mouth.

"Got to get something from my room!" he gasped and ran out. Sophie heard him snorting with laughter as he reached the stairs.

"What's the matter with Max?" said Mum.

"Who knows?' said Sophie. She changed the subject quickly. "So, we can go to Aunty Allie's party then?"

Mum nodded. "Of course. Now, you said you wanted a lift to Cora's house, didn't you?"

"Yes, please," said Sophie. She and the others had arranged to have a

Bridesmaids Club meeting at Cora's
house that afternoon. They were going
to do some planning and then go
shopping for a bridesmaid dress for
Sophie. Aunty Allie had given her some
money and told her to choose something
she really liked. Afterwards they were
going to go to Emily's house for a
decoration-making sleepover. Aunty Allie
had been right – with the wedding in
just over two weeks' time, there wasn't a
second to waste!

"So, let's go through everything. The
invitations have been sent out, haven't

they?" said Shanti, as they all sat on
Cora's bedroom floor. Cora's bedroom
was very different to Shanti's. It was a
lot messier for a start! There was sports
kit scattered across the floor. Her walls
were covered with pictures of horses
and ponies that had been cut out from
magazines. Her duvet had her favourite
football team's emblem on it and she had
some cuddly ponies on her bed.

"Yes, we've invited fifty people,
including all of you, of course," she
said with a grin. One of the best things
about organising the wedding was that
she'd been able to invite the rest of the
Bridesmaids Club!

Shanti checked her list. "Your Aunt Allie has talked to Franketelli's, hasn't she?"

"Yep," said Sophie. "Mr Franketelli was really pleased and said he'll supply champagne for everyone as his present to Mum and Dad. We're going to have pizzas and ice cream for dessert."

"How about the decorations?" said Shanti looking at Emily.

"I've got some good ideas for how we can make the bandstand into a tropical paradise." Emily pulled some pictures that she had printed off the internet out of her bag. "We can start tonight. I've got loads of pink and orange crepe paper

– Dad brought some home from the shop."

"I saw something in one of Mum's magazines about a way to do wedding flowers cheaply," said Sophie. "If you buy bedding plants – those little plants you get in big plastic trays – you can plant them in jam jars and use them as table decorations."

"We can tie pink and orange ribbon around the jars," said Emily. "I've got lots of ribbon at home, too."

"Perfect," said Shanti. "OK, the next thing on my list is getting Sophie a bridesmaid dress."

"Lucie too!" said Sophie. "Aunty Allie

asked me to choose a flower girl outfit for her."

"I'll go and see if Horrible Helena will take us into town," said Cora, getting up.

Sophie wasn't sure why Cora hated Helena so much. They'd met her friend's stepmum-to-be earlier and she had been very friendly. She was very different from Cora, though. Helena ran a fashion company and was very glamorous. Even though it was a Saturday, she was wearing a sparkly jumper, lots of make-up and her hair was carefully curled. When she wasn't at school, Cora wore jeans and a hoodie.

"So, a secret wedding for your parents,

Sophie?" Helena said when they set off for the town centre in her shiny black car. "How amazing!"

Sophie, who was sitting in the front passenger seat as Cora had refused to sit next to Helena, smiled. "I hope they'll be pleased," she said.

"Oh, darling, I bet they'll be over the moon!" said Helena, flicking her hair back. "So, you're off to find a bridesmaid dress?" she said as she parked the car. "Shall I come with? Then I can treat you all to a milkshake afterwards."

"Uh . . . no," said Cora quickly, looking as if she'd rather have her eyes poked out. "We want to go on our own. We'll

see you back here later." She marched
off and a look of disappointment crossed
Helena's face.

"Thanks for bringing us, Helena,"
Emily said politely.

"Yes, it was really kind of you," added
Sophie, feeling bad.

"Well, have fun shopping, girls,"
Helena said almost wistfully.

They ran to catch up with Cora.
"Maybe we should have asked Helena to
come along," Sophie said.

Cora pulled a face. "No way! I don't
want to go shopping with her. It would
be all 'Oh, darling' this and 'Oh, darling'
that." She shuddered. "She's so annoying.

The less time I have to spend with Horrible Helena the better." She glanced round. "So, where should we go first?"

The girls headed into the shopping centre. They had to visit quite a few shops, but at last they found a dress Sophie loved. It was knee-length and made from a dark-pink floaty fabric with a gold ribbon for a belt, and a ruffle round the hem. She found a similar dress for Lucie. Feeling very grown up, she fished her purse out of her bag. "I'll take them both!" she told the sales' assistant.

Later that afternoon, Helena dropped

Sophie back at home with her two bulging carrier bags. They were all going to their houses to collect their sleepover things and then meeting again at Emily's later on.

Sophie let herself into the house, shutting the door quietly behind her. As she tiptoed down the hall, not wanting her parents to see the bags, she heard raised voices. She stopped. Her parents almost never argued.

"For heaven's sake, Tom!" her mum said sharply. "We're going to be in real trouble if you don't get a job soon."

"Do you think I don't know that? But I'm not going to apply just

anywhere!" Dad snapped back.

"Well, maybe you should!" exclaimed Mum. "Just try and get something temporary. Then you can carry on looking for the type of job you would like while earning some money."

"But I don't want to start a job and then leave a few weeks later," Dad argued. "I want to wait and find the right job. You're being unreasonable, Lizzie!"

"And you're living with your head in the clouds!" Mum retorted.

Sophie heard Lucie start to cry.

"We're upsetting Lucie," said Dad. "Come on, sweetpea. Daddy will put

the television on for you."

"Tom, come back! We haven't finished talking about this!" Mum said angrily, as Dad walked out of the kitchen with Lucie in his arms. His hair was sticking up as if he'd been running his hands through it. He stopped abruptly when he saw Sophie.

"Sophie! When did you get in? I didn't hear you."

"I just got here." Sophie felt awkward as her mum appeared behind her dad. She looked upset. Sophie wanted to ask if everything was OK, but she couldn't get the words out. "I'm just getting my sleepover stuff, then I'll go to over to

Emily's house," she muttered.

Her dad nodded. "I'll give you a lift round there if you want." He carried Lucie into the lounge.

Mum gave a forced smile. "Have you had a good time . . . Did you go shopping? What have you got there?"

"Nothing!" Sophie squeaked. She grabbed the bags before her mum could reach them. "Just . . . just some . . . stuff."

"Stuff?" Mum frowned.

"Yes, stuff." Sophie held the bags behind her back. She ran up the stairs, went into her room and hastily hid the bags on top of her wardrobe. *Phew!* That had been close. She had no idea how

she would have explained what she was doing with a bridesmaid dress and a flower girl dress.

I'm going to have to be careful, she thought. *Mum absolutely mustn't find out what we're doing or it will spoil the surprise.* Then she remembered the way her parents had been arguing and unease flickered through her. Her parents both seemed stressed out at the moment. She really hoped she was doing the right thing by organising a secret wedding. *They'll be pleased,* she told herself firmly. *I'm sure they will.*

Chapter Seven

"Do your parents ever argue?" Sophie asked her friends, as they all sat around the kitchen table in Emily's dad's house. They were listening to music and making massive pompoms out of crepe paper. Emily had found a video that showed them how by winding the crepe

paper around large cardboard circles with holes in the middle. They were going to look great!

"My parents row about things like Dad leaving the kitchen in a state, or not putting the bins out, or bringing his bike into the house and leaving mud on the carpet," said Shanti. "He's really messy and Mum gets mad at him, but they usually make up pretty quickly."

"My mum and dad used to have loads of rows before they split up," said Emily. "It was a few years ago now, but I can remember Mum throwing things at Dad when she got angry.

"Dad and Horrible Helena don't

argue, they're too busy kissing all the time." Cora mimed being sick.

"Why are you asking?" Shanti asked Sophie.

She sighed. "No reason, really. It's just . . . well, my mum and dad were arguing when I got in from the shops and they never quarrel normally."

"Don't worry about it," said Shanti quickly. "Like I said, my parents often argue. Lots of parents do."

"Yeah, one fight doesn't mean they're going to split up," said Emily. "My mum and dad were really, really bad before they divorced. They were either arguing or refusing to speak to each other."

"That must have been very hard," said Sophie sympathetically. "I guess mine aren't like that."

"I'm sure they'll be fine. Your dad wouldn't have asked your mum to marry him if they were having problems," said Shanti. "It's probably just the stress of trying to find a new job."

"This wedding will cheer them up!" said Cora

"I really hope so," said Sophie, still feeling a bit worried.

"How can it not?" Emily was

shaking the giant pink pompom she had just finished as if she were a cheerleader. "It's going to be amazing. All their friends will be there, plus you, your little sister, your brother . . ."

"And my aunt, Nana, Grandpa and Gran," added Sophie. Her mum's parents – Nana and Grandpa – lived in France, but had said they would travel over for the wedding. Her dad's mum – Gran – lived right here in Easton. When Sophie had phoned Gran and told her about the secret wedding, she'd thought it was a great idea and had immediately offered to make a cake, just as Sophie had hoped she would.

"It'll be a massive party with all the people they love," said Shanti.

"On the beach where they first met," said Emily.

"With pizzas and ice creams too – what's not to like?" said Cora.

Sophie smiled, feeling much happier.

They made pompoms until they ran out of crepe paper and then made bunting by cutting scraps of orange and pink fabric into triangles. Emily hemmed the edges with her sewing machine so they didn't fray, then they all hand-stitched them on to long lengths of ribbon. When they finally finished, they had four long strings of bunting, plus several boxes of giant pompoms.

"Bedtime!" said Emily, stretching. "Who wants hot chocolate with marshmallows?"

"Me!" they chorused.

They went into the kitchen, made the hot chocolate and then took their mugs upstairs along with a big bowl of extra marshmallows. Emily's room was large and colourful, the walls covered with her drawings and paintings. There was a life-sized papier-mâché dog in one corner and a little wheeled caddy filled with craft supplies. On the floor, there were three air mattresses for Sophie, Cora and Shanti to sleep on.

"Let's play *Never Have I Ever* with marshmallows!" said Cora, as they got changed into their pyjamas.

"How do you play that?" said Sophie.

"One person says, 'never have I ever' and then adds something like 'never have I ever been on a roller coaster', or 'never have I ever used someone else's toothbrush', and then everyone who has done that thing has to eat a marshmallow," said Cora. "I'll start — never have I ever worn someone else's pants!"

They all giggled. "Nope, I've never done that," said Sophie. Emily hadn't either and shook her head, but Shanti

ate a marshmallow. "I was really little!"
she explained. "We went swimming and
I forgot to bring any and my cousin had
a spare pair."

"OK, your turn," said Cora.

"Never have I ever pretended someone
else did something when it was really
me!" said Shanti.

They all ate marshmallows that time.

"OK, how about this one," said
Emily. "Never have I ever been sent a
Valentine's card!"

They all looked round. Sophie ate a
marshmallow. Everyone else squealed.
"Who sent it ?" gasped Emily. "Do you
know?"

"Yep!" Sophie grinned. "It was my little brother, Max."

They all groaned and Cora threw a marshmallow at her.

By the time all the marshmallows had gone, they weren't sleepy at all. "Pillow fight!" cried Cora. She grabbed a pillow and hit Sophie over the head with it. "Got you!"

Sophie grabbed hers and hit Cora just as hard. "Got you back!"

Emily and Shanti joined in and soon they were all squealing and laughing. They didn't stop until Emily's dad opened the bedroom door. "Whatever is going on, girls? It sounds like there's a

troupe of monkeys up here!"

Cora let go of the pillow she was aiming at Emily and it flew through the air, hitting Emily's dad. She covered her mouth with her hands. "I'm really sorry!"

Luckily, Emily's dad wasn't cross. "Hmm. I think it's brushing teeth and bed time."

A little while later, they were all snuggled down in their sleeping bags with the light off. Sophie sighed happily. This had been the best sleepover ever. She couldn't believe that in two weeks it was going to be her parents' wedding. *Will Mum and Dad really be happy with the surprise?* wondered Sophie. Her friends

were convinced that Sophie's parents would love it, and she hoped with all her heart that they were right!

Chapter Eight

Over the next week, Bridesmaids Club met whenever they could after school, making more pompoms and bunting. They also collected and washed jam jars and on Friday, Aunty Allie took a trip to a garden centre and dropped lots of plastic trays with bright yellow,

orange and pink plants off at Emily's mum's house. The girls sat in the sun in the large garden and planted pansies in the jam jars to make table decorations. Emily's mum had said they could use any flowers they liked from her garden for Sophie's mum's bouquet, but they weren't going to pick those until the last moment.

The flowers and decorations are sorted, the food is sorted, the music is sorted and Aunty Allie's booked someone to conduct the wedding, Sophie thought to herself as she cycled home. *Gran's making the cake and I'm going to help her ice it. I've got my bridesmaid dress and Lucie's flower girl dress. Mum's got her*

wedding dress. Everything's under control.

When she got in, she headed up to her room. Mum's car was out – she was putting in extra hours at work. Dad was bathing Lucie. As Sophie passed Max's bedroom door he called to her, "Hey, Sophie! Come and look at my new trick. It'll be perfect for the—"

"Ssh, you doughnut!" Sophie hurried into his room and shut the door. "Dad might hear!"

Max grinned. "Sorry! Well, I've been practising loads of tricks. I've got this one with these rings." He picked up two large metal rings, each the size of a dinner plate.

"Rings!" gasped Sophie, her hand flying to her mouth.

Max look puzzled. "Yeah, these are rings."

"No, wedding rings!" Sophie exclaimed.

"These aren't wedding rings," said Max, looking at her as if he thought she was mad. "They're much too big."

"Duh! I know that," Sophie said. "No, what I meant was, we haven't got any wedding rings. What are we going to do, Max? Rings are expensive, we can't just go and buy them."

Max shrugged. "I dunno."

Sophie rubbed her forehead. "OK,

I need to think about this."

"What am I going to wear?" Max asked suddenly. "I should wear something smart, shouldn't I? But I've only got jeans or my football kit or my school uniform."

Sophie stared at him. In her excitement about the bridesmaids' dresses, she'd completely forgotten that Max would need something to wear too! "I really don't know," she said. What else had she forgotten?

Just then Max's door opened. "I thought I heard you come in, Sophie," said Dad. He had Lucie on his hip. "What are you up to in here, you two?"

"Nothing!" they both said quickly. Sophie cringed. They sounded like they were trying to hide something. Luckily, Dad didn't seem to notice. "I've got a job interview tomorrow morning and so I've made some cupcakes to celebrate. I thought we could decorate them, so they'll be ready when your mum gets home from work."

"What's the job, Dad?" Sophie asked, as they went downstairs.

"It's managing a pub in a village out of town," Dad said. "It's not exactly what I wanted – I'd much rather be managing a restaurant, and it's forty minutes away so more time travelling – but they want

someone who can start straight away. There's only me and one other person being interviewed, and I get the feeling I'm their first choice."

"I bet they'll offer you the job!" said Max.

"I hope so!" said Dad.

They went into the kitchen, where a big batch of chocolate cupcakes was cooling on a wire rack. "Yum!" said Max.

Sophie blinked. "It's a bit of a mess in here, Dad." There were dirty mixing bowls and baking trays in the sink, and flour and sugar covered the work surfaces.

"We can clear up once we've
decorated the cakes," said Dad. "But
first we need to make some chocolate
frosting. Max, you get the icing sugar
and cocoa powder. Soph, you get the
butter and another mixing bowl, and I'll
get the icing bags ready. Let's go, team!"

They made loads of frosting and had

great fun decorating the cupcakes. The piping bags were hard to use and frosting kept landing on the table, so in the end they just spooned thick dollops of icing on top of the cakes and smoothed it over. They gave Lucie one of the spoons to lick and soon her face, hair and sleepsuit were covered in creamy chocolate.

"She's going to need another bath!" Max grinned, licking frosting of his fingers.

"I think we'll all need baths tonight!" said Sophie, looking at the splodges in Max's hair.

Just then, there was the sound of the front door opening and a few moments

later, Mum came into the kitchen. She looked tired.

"Mama!" cried Lucie, waving the spoon at her.

"Hi, Mum," called Max. "Look at our cakes!"

Mum's forehead furrowed into a frown as she glanced around the kitchen. "Tom," she said slowly. "What's going on?"

Uh-oh, thought Sophie, seeing how tense Mum's face was.

Her dad recognised the danger signs too. "I know it's a bit of a mess, Lizzie, but I'll clear it up. Don't stress."

"Don't stress?" Mum echoed. Her hand

flew to her forehead. "Lucie's covered in chocolate, it's well past her bedtime and Sophie and Max appear to be eating chocolate cake for their tea!" Her voice rose. "And the kitchen – the kitchen I left clean and tidy this morning before I went out to work – now looks like a bomb site! What is going on?"

"Lizzie, please just sit down. You look shattered," Dad said.

Mum exploded. "That's because I *am* shattered, Tom! I'm working all hours trying to bring in enough money to keep us going while you sit around waiting for the perfect job to drop in your lap. In the meantime, you can't even keep the

house tidy, feed the children tea and get the baby into bed on time!"

Lucie dropped the spoon and started to howl.

"You're overreacting! So what if there's some washing up to do and Lucie's missed her bedtime?" Dad exclaimed. "The kids are all happy. Or they were until you walked in!"

Mum shut her mouth with a snap and swung round.

"Mum! Wait!" Sophie dashed in front of her. "Dad didn't mean that. We are happy you're here. And he hasn't been sitting round all day. He's got a job interview tomorrow." She looked at her mum desperately, hating the fact her parents were arguing. "He's bound to get it and it starts right away."

"What interview?" said Mum, looking across at Dad.

"Sit down and I'll tell you," said Dad, more quietly. "Then I'll put Lucie to bed and clear up."

Mum took a deep breath and sat down at the table. While Dad told her about his job interview, Sophie cleaned Lucie up at the sink and Max cleared away the dirty bowls.

"I think I have a good chance of getting it," Dad finished.

Mum nodded slowly. "You've got an

excellent chance. You've been in the business twenty years, you're brilliant with customers and got great references."

"You'll get it, Dad. I know you will!" said Sophie encouragingly.

Dad put his arm around Mum's shoulders. "By tomorrow I should be employed again. It's going to be all right, Lizzie. You'll see."

Mum smiled, but as she rested her head against his shoulder, Sophie saw the worry in her eyes.

Later that night, Sophie lay in bed thinking about the problem of the

wedding rings. They couldn't borrow them. Once you gave someone a wedding ring, it was theirs to keep. What was she going to do?

There was a knock at her bedroom door. "It's me, Max," Max hissed from the other side of the door. "I've had an idea about what I can wear for you-know-what. Can I come in?"

"Sure," Sophie said quickly.

The door opened and Max jumped in wearing his magician's outfit

– a top hat and a black cloak with a red waistcoat, and his newest school trousers. "Ta-da!" he said.

Sophie stared. Max looked smart. He was going to do conjuring tricks and it was a perfect outfit for that. And best men often wore top hats.

"Well?" Max said eagerly. "What do you think?"

Sophie leapt up from bed and hugged him. "I think it's brilliant!" she said.

He beamed in delight.

"Another problem solved," said Sophie.

"Just the wedding rings to work out," said Max.

"Yes, just the wedding rings," agreed

Sophie, wishing her brother could magic
some out of thin air.

The next afternoon, Sophie sat in her
gran's kitchen, helping to pour ganache
– a thick chocolate coating – on to the
three-tiered wedding cake her gran had
made. Sophie had found a picture of
a cake on the internet. It had a shiny
coating of dark chocolate ganache
and was decorated with violet and
white flowers made from sugar paste.
Sophie and her gran were going to do
something similar, but with bright pink
and orange flowers. As they worked

together, coating the cakes with the
ganache and adding food colouring to
the sugar paste, Sophie filled Gran in on
everything to do with the wedding. "I
don't know what I'm going to do about
the rings," she finished.

"You know, I may be able to help
you," said Gran. "Wait here."

She went upstairs and a few minutes
later returned with a red leather
jewellery box. "Here," she said. "Look
inside."

Sophie opened it and saw two gold
wedding rings.

"They were mine and your grandad's,"
said Gran. "I can't wear mine anymore.

Not with my arthritis. It's daft them sitting here in this box. You can have them for your mum and dad."

"Really?" gasped Sophie.

Gran smiled. "Really. Your grandad and I were happily married for fifty years. I hope they'll bring your mum and dad just as many happy years together."

Sophie hugged her. "Thank you, Gran! That's the last problem solved!"

They finished decorating the cake and then Gran dropped her back at home. Sophie hurried inside feeling excited. Everything was really starting to come together.

Max was in the lounge playing trains with Lucie, and Mum was in the kitchen going through a spreadsheet of figures on her laptop. "Hi," said Sophie, looking round the kitchen door.

"Hi, sweetie," said Mum. "Did you have a nice time at Gran's?"

"Yes, thanks," said Sophie.

"What were you doing?" Mum asked.

"Oh, just a bit of baking," said Sophie. "Have you heard from Dad?"

"No," said Mum, frowning. "I thought he'd be back a while ago. I've tried ringing and texting, but he's not answering."

"Maybe they offered him the job and

he stayed to find out more about it,"
Sophie suggested.

"I hope so," said Mum.

Just then there was the sound of the
back door opening and Dad came in.
His hair was rumpled, his tie crooked
and he had an oil stain on the front
of his shirt. "What happened to you?"
Mum said in surprise. "You look like
you've been dragged through a hedge
backwards!"

"Did you get the job?" Sophie asked
eagerly.

Dad shook his head. "No. The car
broke down on the way to the interview."

"Oh no!" exclaimed Mum. "Did you

ring them and explain?"

"I couldn't," said Dad. "I was in such a rush when I left the house, I forgot my phone."

"You left your phone here?" echoed Mum. "Tom!"

Dad nodded. "I know. It meant I couldn't phone roadside assistance. I was in the middle of nowhere and had to walk five miles until I got to a village. By then I'd missed the interview and because I'd not shown up, they gave the job to the other person." He looked at Mum. "I'm sorry, Lizzie."

Sophie could see how upset her dad looked. She went over and hugged him.

"Never mind, Dad. There'll be other jobs."

"Thanks, Soph," he said ruefully.

"What about the car?" Mum said.

Dad hesitated. "It's not good news. It's the steering. The breakdown mechanic reckons it will cost a few thousand to repair."

Sophie saw her mum swallow. "A few thousand?" she echoed. "Well, that's it then," she said sharply. "We'd better forget all about having a wedding. We're going to have to use our savings to fix the car." She shook her head. "I'll take my dress back to the shop and get the money back."

"There's no need to do that, Lizzie," said Dad, going over and squeezing her shoulder. "We're just delaying the wedding, not abandoning the idea completely."

"No," Mum said, jumping to her feet angrily. "We might as well accept it, Tom. This wedding is not going to happen. This time it's the car, but next time it will be something else. No doubt I'll have to sort it out, just like I always have to sort everything out!" She took her engagement ring off. "We might as well sell this too."

"Lizzie!" Dad protested.

"Why not? I don't need a ring. *We're*

not getting married. End of story." Mum marched out of the room.

Sophie glanced anxiously at her dad. "Are you going to go after her?"

He shook his head. "I know your mum. She needs time to calm down. And if she's made up her mind, she won't change it no matter what I say. I'm sorry, Soph." He rubbed his forehead unhappily. "I guess the wedding really is off – for good!"

Chapter Nine

"What am I going to do?" Sophie said
to her friends. She'd called an emergency
Bridesmaids Club meeting. "Mum's
given Dad his engagement ring back.
She says they're never getting married.
Do you think I should just cancel the
wedding?" said Sophie. "I mean, what if

Mum refuses to marry Dad in front of everyone?"

"That won't happen," said Cora, but she didn't sound certain.

Sophie groaned. "I don't know what to do!"

"It'll be OK," said Shanti, reassuringly. "I bet your mum will be fine on the day."

"Shanti's right. Your mum and dad will get married and it'll all be great," added Emily.

Sophie looked anxiously at her friends. She wanted to believe them, she really did. But what if Mum meant what she'd said about not getting married?

What would she say when she turned up and found herself at her own surprise wedding? Remembering how angry her mum was last night, Sophie wasn't sure she wanted to find out!

Aunty Allie agreed with Cora, Emily and Shanti. "Your mum was just tired and cross," she said when Sophie told her what had happened. "I'm sure she didn't mean what she said. She loves your dad. I think we should go ahead and hope for the best."

"But what about the dress?" said Sophie. "She's going to return it."

"Don't worry. I'll offer to return it to the shop for her because she's so busy, but instead I'll keep it. And one of the guys in Zayne's band is a mechanic. I'll get him to have a look at the car. I bet he can fix it more cheaply so they won't need the money from the dress."

"OK," said Sophie. "Oh, Aunty Allie, I hope this all works out."

"Me too!" said Aunty Allie, giving Sophie a hug.

As the week went by, Sophie's anxiety grew. Mum was working very long hours and when she came home, she was too

tired to do much apart from fall asleep on the sofa. Dad was trying to keep the house tidy and was looking through job websites every day, but he was much quieter than usual and seemed to be tiptoeing around Mum. By the morning of the wedding, Sophie felt as tense as a balloon blown to bursting point. She woke up very early, just as the sun was rising in the bright blue sky.

What are we doing? she thought, feeling sick. *Why did I ever think a surprise wedding would be a good idea? What if it's a disaster?*

Her phone buzzed. It was a text from Shanti. R U OK? Don't worry – it's going to be the best wedding ever. Hugs. xxx

Thx! Sophie replied, sending three fingers crossed emojis.

One of the best things about setting up Bridesmaids Club had been getting to know Shanti better. She was really kind and Sophie felt like she could talk to her about anything. She really liked Cora and Emily, too. As she ate her cereal that morning, they all started to message her on the group chat they'd set up.

It's a perfect day for a WEDDING! What time are we meeting at Em's? That was from Cora.

9.30 so we can pick the flowers and make the bouquet, Shanti replied. **Sophie and her aunt are going to take**

the cake to Franketelli's together with the wedding clothes. We'll meet them there at 11 to help set up.

Dad can give us a lift 2 the restaurant, Emily wrote. The decorations are in the boot of his car already.

EXCITING!!! typed Cora sending a string of exploding fireworks.

And terrifying, Sophie wrote, sending a scared face.

IT WILL BE GR8! typed Shanti.

Bridesmaids Club will make sure of it! added Cora.

As Sophie put her cereal bowl in the dishwasher, Max came into the kitchen.

He was wearing his magician's outfit.
"Today's the day!" he said excitedly. He
took off his top hat and pulled a bunch
of fake flowers out of it. "Marry me,
Sophie!" he said, sinking to one knee and
thrusting the flowers into her face.

Despite her anxiety, Sophie grinned
and shut the door behind him. "You
doughnut! Now, are you sure you know
what you've got to do?"

"Yep," he said nodding hard. "I've got
to get Mum and Dad and Lucie to the
beach at five o'clock."

"That's right. The . . ." Sophie
lowered her voice despite the shut door,
"wedding's at six o'clock just as the sun

begins to set. Aunty Allie asked Mum
and Dad to come to her 'birthday party'
a bit earlier than the other guests. She
told them she needs a hand getting
ready. That'll give Mum and Lucie the
chance to get changed when they realise
it's not a birthday party after all!"

"So, what are you doing today?" Max
asked.

"Aunty Allie's picking me up in
ten minutes and we're going to set
everything up," said Sophie. "I've told
Mum and Dad I'm helping her decorate
for her birthday party."

A few minutes later, Aunty Allie
honked her horn outside the house.

Sophie hurried out of her bedroom with the carrier bags containing the dresses and almost bumped straight into Mum who was coming out of Lucie's room.

"Mum!" Sophie gasped, shoving the carrier bags behind her back.

Mum looked at her curiously. "Are you OK?"

Sophie nodded hard. "Yeah." She said, her voice rising. "Of course I am! Why wouldn't I be?"

Luckily at that moment, Lucie toddled to the door. "Mama! Story!" she demanded, waving a book about trains. "Story now!"

Mum turned her attention to Lucie

and Sophie saw her chance. She scooted past. "See you later!" she called and she raced down the stairs. Her heart was pounding in her chest. *Phew!* That had been close!

She jumped into her aunt's car. "Got everything?" Aunty Allie said.

"Yep!" said Sophie, feeling like she'd just escaped after a bank robbery. "Let's go!"

They picked the cake up from Gran's house, then drove straight to the restaurant. Mr Franketelli was waiting for them outside. "Come in! Come in!" he said, ushering Sophie and Aunty Allie inside where the tables were covered

with clean white tablecloths. His eyes twinkled in his lined face. "The wedding? It is still a *segreto* – a secret?"

"Yes!" said Sophie.

Mr Franketelli kissed the tips of his fingers. "*Bravo!* We will make it the best wedding ever!" He turned to Sophie. "And your papa? How is he?"

"Not great. He hasn't got a job at the moment. Did you hear about The Wellington closing down?" she said.

Mr Franketelli nodded. "I did. So, he has not found a new job yet?"

"No, not yet," admitted Sophie.

"Ah, poor man," said Mr Franketelli, shaking his head. "Well, today, we shall give him a good day – a great day – that he will always remember!"

Sophie smiled. "Thanks, Mr Franketelli!"

They unloaded the cake and dresses from Aunty Allie's car and then the others arrived. They piled out of Emily's dad's car with the decorations and set to work too. They tied the pompoms around the room and hung up a banner that Emily had made

saying CONGRATULATIONS! She'd decorated it with pink, orange and yellow flowers. They put a pansy-filled jam jar in the middle of each table and hung up the bunting.

Aunty Allie hung the dresses up in Mr Franketelli's office. There were old menus, files and folders piled high on the desk. "I am sorry for the mess," said Mr Franketelli apologetically. "I always mean to tidy and never have the time. Running a restaurant . . ." He rubbed his forehead. "It is a young person's job."

After lunch, Aunty Allie's boyfriend, Zayne, arrived in a van with his two friends, Mo and Andy, who were also

in his band. "Hello, titch," Zayne said to Sophie. It was what he always called her. He was very tall with spiky dark hair. "So, today's the big day for your parents?"

Sophie nodded. "I hope it's going to be OK."

Zayne frowned. "It's brave. I'll give you that. I'm not sure I'd want a surprise wedding."

"Not helpful, Zayne!" Aunty Allie cried, swiping him round the head.

"Hey, what do I know? Ignore me. It'll be fine!" Zayne said with a grin. He and the others set to work unloading their guitars, keyboard, drums and speakers

and set the equipment up in one corner of the restaurant.

Meanwhile, the girls decorated the bandstand. It was at the end of a short pier that jutted out from the promenade, just opposite the restaurant. The bandstand was made of bluey-green metal – eight ornate pillars held up a canopy that looked a bit like a pointy hat. The girls hung bunting and bright pompoms around the iron frame and put two large pots of flowers from Emily's mum's garden at the entrance.

Zayne headed off in the van and returned with folding chairs. The girls and Aunty Allie put them in rows outside

the bandstand for the guests to sit on.
As a final finishing touch, they wound
strings of battery-operated fairy lights
around the bandstand's pillars.

"I guess Horrible Helena's good for
something, after all," said Cora. The fairy
lights had come from the spare room her
future stepmum used as a yoga studio.
When she'd heard that Sophie's parents
were getting married in the bandstand,
she'd suggested that the girls borrow
them.

"I think we're all done," said Sophie at
last. The bandstand looked wonderfully
romantic with the twinkling fairy lights
adding extra magic and sparkle.

"It looks beautiful!" said Emily.

"Your mum and dad are going to be here soon!" said Aunty Allie, checking the time on her phone.

Sophie felt a rush of nerves. "It was the right thing to do, wasn't it – organising a surprise wedding?" she said anxiously.

"Yes!" Shanti said. "Your mum and dad are going to be so happy!"

Butterflies fluttered in Sophie's tummy. Was Shanti right? *We're not getting married. End of story.* Her mum's words echoed in Sophie's head.

Cora grabbed her arm excitedly. "Sophie! They're here!"

Sophie swung round. Max was holding

Mum's hand, grinning and pulling
her along the promenade, towards the
bandstand. Dad, who was wearing his
best suit for the party, was following with
Lucie on his shoulders.

Aunty Allie took a deep breath. "Here
we go," she whispered. Glancing up at
her, Sophie suddenly realised her aunt
was as worried as she was.

Mum's eyes widened as she got closer.
"Wow, Allie! This is some birthday
party!" she said. "It looks like it's ready
for a wedding!"

There was a long pause. Sophie licked
her suddenly dry lips. "It *is* ready for a
wedding," she said. "Mum, Dad – it's

all ready for your wedding."

She saw the confusion on her parents' faces. "What?" Mum said.

Max jumped up and down on the spot, unable to contain his excitement any longer. "We knew you wanted to have an amazing beach wedding, but couldn't afford it, so we made one for you. It was Sophie's idea! I'm the best man and she's the bridesmaid!"

"It's true," said Aunty Allie, taking Mum's hands. "Sophie and her friends have organised it all."

"We're the Bridesmaids Club," said Cora helpfully.

"They've arranged it so you can

have your beach wedding right here in Easton!" said Aunty Allie. "The guests will be arriving in an hour."

Sophie could hardly breathe. Dad was beaming but her mum looked stunned. "Mum?" Sophie said anxiously.

To her horror, her mum put her face in her hands and burst into tears.

Chapter Ten

"Mum?" said Sophie in alarm. This was NOT how she had imagined this going. She hadn't meant to make her mum cry.

"Lizzie?" said her dad, handing Lucie quickly to Aunty Allie and pulling Mum into a hug. "Please don't cry. The kids meant to help, but if you don't want to

get married that's fine. Absolutely fine. We can call it all off."

"Don't be upset, Mum!" Max begged.

Mum looked up. "But I'm not upset." She dashed her tears away with her hands. "I'm crying because I'm happy. I can't believe you did all this and kept it secret," she said to Sophie. She looked around at the bandstand "It's incredible."

"It wasn't just me. It was Shanti, Emily and Cora too,' said Sophie. They all grinned. "Aunty Allie as well. In fact, lots of people helped – Gran, Mr Franketelli, Zayne. Are you sure it's OK though? You don't have to get married if you don't want to."

"Of course I want to!" said Mum. "A wedding doesn't need to be expensive and fancy. The only important thing is . . ." she took a breath, "that you are marrying the person you love most in the world."

She pulled away from Dad and knelt down on one knee. "Tom, you asked me this before, now it's my turn to ask you . . . Will you marry me?" she said.

There was a moment's pause then Dad grinned. "You bet!"

He grabbed her hand, then picked her up and swung her round. "What are you doing?" she shrieked.

"This!" he said, kissing her. "We're finally getting married, Lizzie!" He whooped. "Right where we first met!"

"In less than an hour!" said Sophie.

"Oh my gosh!" said Mum, looking stunned. "What am I going to wear?

"I didn't return your dress," said Aunty Allie. "It's at Franketelli's, all ready for you to get changed into."

Sophie grinned. "What are we waiting for, Mum? You've got a wedding to go to!"

Cora, Emily and Shanti changed into their wedding outfits in the restaurant cloakroom. Shanti and Emily were wearing dresses and Cora had a red top with embroidered butterflies over smart black jeans. When they were ready, they went outside with Max to greet the guests and show them to their seats.

Meanwhile, Mum and Dad met the celebrant – a lady called Nancy who was going to marry them and make it all official – and had a chat with her. Then Mum, Sophie, and Lucie went inside to get ready. Sophie put on her dress and then helped Lucie put on her matching one. When they were both

dressed, Sophie picked up her little sister and twirled around, making Lucie giggle. As her skirt swirled out around her, Sophie felt a shiver of excitement. She loved her dress!

Sophie took Lucie outside, leaving Aunty Allie to help Mum put the finishing touches to her make-up. Dad was chatting to Mr Franketelli and thanking him for all his help. "If there's anything I can do in return, do let me know. I'm not working at the moment so I'm more than happy to help you out for a few weeks. Let you and Gina have some time off, take a holiday. I really appreciate you letting us hold

the wedding reception here."

"My pleasure," Mr Franketelli nodded, his eyes thoughtful. "You know, there may be something you can do for me but we shall talk about that later. For now, you have guests to greet." He caught sight of Sophie and Lucie. "Ah, *bellisima!*" he said, his eyes shining.

"You look beautiful, both of you," said Dad, coming over.

Sophie twirled. "You like our dresses then?"

Lucie tried to copy her and fell over. "Whoopsie!" she said.

Dad laughed and scooped her up. "The perfect bridesmaid and the perfect flower

girl!" He bent down and dropped a kiss on Sophie's head. "I can't believe you did all this, Soph."

Sophie smiled up at him. "I'm just glad Mum didn't freak out and run away when I told her what was going on!"

Dad chuckled. "Me too! You're a braver person than me!"

They went outside. Nancy was in the bandstand and the guests were arriving. Dad greeted them all. He loved talking to people and making everyone feel welcome. Max came running up to Sophie. "Look! I've got the rings!" he said pulling them out of his pocket. "Gran gave them to me."

"Brilliant," said Sophie. "Keep them
safe. You'll need to get them out when
Nancy asks for them."

Aunty Allie hurried over. "Your mum's
ready and waiting, Sophie," she said.
"I'll look after Lucie. She's a bit too little
to walk behind your mum." She picked
Lucie up and joined Zayne and Gran in
the front row. Then she pressed a button
on her phone and wedding music began
to play out of the portable speakers
that had been set up in the bandstand.
Realising the wedding was about to
start, all the guests took their seats.

"This is it!" Cora said to Sophie.
"You're actually about to be a

bridesmaid!" squealed Emily.

"Good luck!" said Shanti.

"Thanks, guys. You're the best!" said
Sophie. She ran into Franketelli's where
her mum was waiting for her. She looked
gorgeous! The wedding dress fit her
perfectly and the tiara sparkled in her
hair, holding her veil in place. "You look
beautiful," Sophie said.

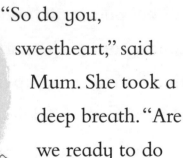

"So do you,
sweetheart," said
Mum. She took a
deep breath. "Are
we ready to do
this?"

Sophie nodded

and went behind her to pick up the long train. "Ready when you are!" she said.

As Mum stepped out of Franketelli's, Aunty Allie changed the music to the traditional wedding march. Mum walked slowly down the pier towards the bandstand with Sophie holding up her train. Everyone smiled as they passed, but the girls from Bridesmaids Club were grinning widest of all. Catching her friends' eyes, Sophie felt so proud and happy she thought she might burst! When they reached the front, Sophie carefully arranged the train around Mum so it looked perfect, then stood to the side with Aunty Allie and Max. Dad

was gazing at Mum as if he couldn't take his eyes off her. The sun was just beginning to set, pink and gold streaking across the sky, as the wedding began.

After Nancy had welcomed everyone, Mum and Dad had to say their marriage vows, agreeing to be husband and wife and promising to love and cherish each other for as long as they lived. When it was time for them to exchange the wedding rings, Max held out the gold rings that Gran had given to Sophie. Mum's hand flew to her mouth and her eyes shone with tears.

"Don't cry, Mum!" Max said in alarm. "Here, take this." He pulled a red hanky

178

out of his pocket. It was quickly followed by a green one, then a blue one, then a pink one. "Oh, said Max in alarm, looking at the string of hankies. "That trick was supposed to happen later!"

Everyone burst out laughing, including Mum.

"Magic, pure magic!" chuckled Dad.

Mum mopped her eyes with the string of hankies and then she and Dad exchanged rings and kissed. They were now officially husband and wife!

Once the ceremony was over, Mr Franketelli brought out champagne glasses and handed them round.

"Here. I'll do that!" said Dad, sweeping

the tray of drinks off him.

Mr Franketelli chuckled. "Your papa," he said to Sophie. "He's good at this, isn't he?"

"Oh, yes," she said. "He loves looking after people. He hates not having a job." Mr Franketelli nodded understandingly.

Once everyone had a glass of champagne, Dad clapped his hands. "Thank you all for joining us. It's been an incredible day. So emotional that even the cake is in tiers!" Everyone groaned. Dad grinned. "Now, before we go inside to eat, I would like to say some thank yous. First to my gorgeous new wife for putting up with me through

good times and bad. You really are the best mother and partner in the world, and I will love you as long as I live."

He raised his champagne glass to Mum and everyone said, "Ahhhh."

"Next, to the best sister-in-law anyone could hope to have," Dad carried on. "Allie, I know this wedding would not have happened without your help, so thank you. To Zayne, the Franketelli family and to my best man and best son in the world, Max. To lovely little Lucie, for not dribbling on my suit. You are all wonderful."

Everyone clapped and then Dad raised his glass again. "Last, but most certainly

not least," he said, "the biggest thank you goes to my amazing daughter, Sophie, and her friends, Cora, Emily and Shanti who together make up the Bridesmaids Club. I understand that the four of you planned this wedding and did most of the organising. You've showed everyone here that with determination, imagination and team work, anything is possible." He raised his glass. "To the brilliant Bridesmaids Club!"

Everyone cheered and Sophie's friends surrounded her in a group hug.

"And now it's time for something even cheesier than me – it's pizza time!" said Dad with a grin.

After everyone had eaten as much pizza and ice cream as they could, Mum and Dad cut the cake. While the slices were being handed round, Max did a magic show. He conjured coins from people's ears, made two rings connect and come apart, produced a bunch of flowers out of his top hat and pulled endless hankies from his pockets. Everyone clapped and cheered.

As the tables were being pushed back to make room for dancing, Mr Franketelli came over to Sophie and her parents. "It has been a good day then?"

he asked them, smiling broadly.

"The best!" Mum said.

Dad nodded. "Remember what I said, Antonio. If I can do you a favour, then just ask."

"Well," said Mr Franketelli, looking thoughtful. "That's what I would like to talk to you about, Tom. I've been thinking about retiring for some time, but there has never been anyone I would trust to run Franketelli's. You, my friend – I would trust you. Would you consider becoming my restaurant manager?"

Dad stared. "What? Work here?"

"Think about it, at least," said Mr Franketelli. He shrugged. "I know you

are used to working at a fancier place and you may not want to run a simple Italian restaurant . . ."

"But I do!" Dad interrupted. "I would love to manage Franketelli's. This is the perfect place for me."

"It really is!" gasped Sophie, thinking how amazing it would be to have her dad working here. They'd get free ice cream whenever they wanted it!

Mum took Mr Franketelli's hands and kissed him on both cheeks. "Oh, Mr Franketelli, thank you! This really is the perfect end to the perfect day!"

Mr Franketelli beamed. "*Magnifico!* We will talk more tomorrow, but for now, enjoy the evening, my friends!"

Zayne's band began to play. Dad grabbed Mum by the hand and pulled her out to dance. Sophie and her friends charged on to the dance floor too, while Aunty Allie waltzed Lucie around the room, and Max pulled Gran up from her chair. Soon everyone was up on their feet, moving to the music.

"This is brilliant!" whooped Cora.

"I can't believe our first wedding has gone so well!" said Shanti.

"And there are still three more to go!" said Emily.

"Bridesmaids Club rules!" said Sophie. Sophie felt like she was going to

explode with happiness. Her mum and dad were married. Her dad had a new job and she had the three best friends ever.

"I love weddings!" she exclaimed.

"We all do!" cried Shanti.

Then, as fairy lights twinkled and the sound of music and laughter floated up into the moonlit sky, the four Bridesmaids Club friends danced the night away.

The End

Save the date!

Read on for a sneak peak of Shanti's story . . .

"So, now I've been a bridesmaid, it's your turn next," Sophie said to Shanti.

"It's just a week now until Rekha's wedding, isn't it?" said Emily.

Shanti nodded. Rekha was her older sister and the wedding celebrations were starting on Saturday – in six days' time. She looked over at the beautiful pink bridesmaid *lehenga* hanging on her wardrobe door. "I really can't wait. It's going to be so much fun," she said, her brown eyes shining.

"What happens at an Indian wedding?" asked Cora curiously.

"Well, I've only been to one and that was when I was really little so I don't remember it very well," admitted Shanti. Her mum's family was originally from northern India. She had grown up there and had come over to England when she was eighteen, but Shanti's dad had been born in the UK. Shanti had been very surprised when her sister had said she wanted to have a big Indian wedding, but her husband-to-be came from a much more traditional family.

"It's not just one single ceremony like at Sophie's mum and dad's wedding," Shanti went on. "But lots of different celebrations. We've already had one big party at Ansh's house – kind of an engagement party. For the wedding itself, there'll be lots of ceremonies and lots of eating, dancing and partying for three days. We've got relatives coming from all over the place. Nani – that's my mum's mother – is coming all the way from India. She's arriving tonight and staying here until after the wedding. Mum's really stressing out about it because Nani hasn't been to visit since I was three. Mum says Nani's really traditional and we're just not. I hope it's all OK . . . "

To find out what happens next, read
Big Bollywood Wedding!

Beach Wedding Bliss

Posy Diamond

With special thanks to Linda Chapman.

ORCHARD BOOKS

First published in Great Britain in 2020 by The Watts Publishing Group

1 3 5 7 9 10 8 6 4 2

Text copyright © Orchard Books 2020
Illustrations copyright © Orchard Books 2020
The moral rights of the author and illustrator have been asserted.

A CIP catalogue record for this book
is available from the British Library.

ISBN 978 1 40836 085 9

Printed and bound in Great Britain by Clays Ltd, Elcograf S.p.A

The paper and board used in this book are made from wood from responsible sources.

Orchard Books
An imprint of
Hachette Children's Group
Part of The Watts Publishing Group Limited
Carmelite House
50 Victoria Embankment
London EC4Y 0DZ

An Hachette UK Company
www.hachette.co.uk
www.hachettechildrens.co.uk